Steve Breen

A PERFECT MESS

DIAL BOOKS FOR YOUNG READERS

To Jane and Cate

DIAL BOOKS FOR YOUNG READERS • Penguin Young Readers Group
An imprint of Penguin Random House LLC • 375 Hudson Street, New York, NY 10014

Copyright © 2016 by Steve Breen

Printed in China • ISBN: 978-0-8037-4156-0
1 3 5 7 9 10 8 6 4 2
Designed by Jason Henry • Text set in Providence
The artwork for this book was created with ink pens,
watercolors, and colored pencils..

Grass
stains

Chain-link fence
rust

Spaghetti
sauce

Staying clean isn't easy.

Dirt

Chocolate milk

Jelly

Mustard

Pancake syrup

Mud

Gum

And most days,

7:23 am

Henry didn't mind being messy one bit.

7:25 AM

But when he woke up Tuesday morning,
he vowed that things would be different.

"I've picked out your nicest shirt for school today. Please try your best to keep it clean," Mom said.

"I will," Henry promised.

For breakfast, Henry ate the whitest
food in the fridge.

He even wore his little sister's bib.

Henry's mom handed him a packet of wipes "just in case" as he headed out the door.

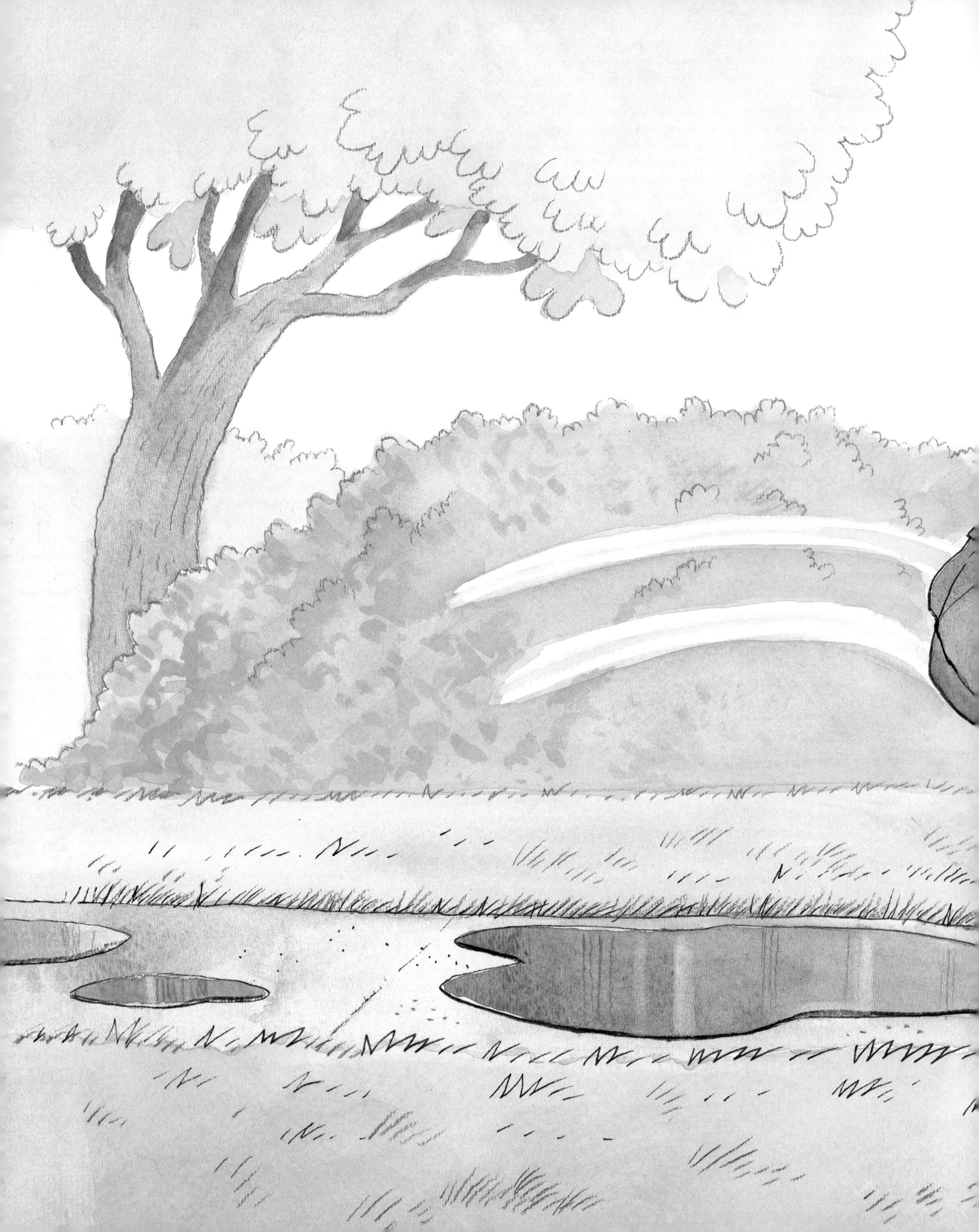

Henry carefully jumped over every muddy
puddle on his way to the bus stop.

Sam passed Henry a jelly donut. But Henry handed it right back . . . just as the bus hit a pothole.

Whoops!

During art class, Henry was worried about spilling paint. So he asked Mrs. Williams's permission to sit in the back of the room.

At snack time, Henry chose water instead of grape juice and cookies. But he tripped on Gordon's back pack.

"Excuse me," Henry said.

When he sat down to write an apology note,
his pen stopped working. So he shook it.

By that afternoon, the whole class had had a "run-in" with Henry. But Henry had stayed perfectly clean.

Then Mrs. Williams lined everyone up.
"Come on, class, follow me," she said.

They walked to the gym and took their places in front of the camera.

"Class picture time!" Henry's teacher said.

Henry beamed the whitest and brightest.
That is, until someone yelled . . .

MRS. WILLIAMS
KINDERGARTEN

"GROUP HUG!"

And everyone grabbed Henry.

Henry may not have stayed perfectly clean . . . but he and his friends were perfectly happy at the end of the day.